Bismillah Al Rahman Al Rahim

FINDERS KEEPERS & OTHER STORIES

By

Qasim Najar

&

Samina Najar

New York

Finders
Keepers
and Other Stories

Qasim Najar and Samina Najar

Editing and proof reading provided by: Samina Baig
Design Consultant: Yahiya Emerick
Cover Design: Tariq Khan

First print: July 1998

Published and distributed by:
International Books & Tapes Supply
PO Box 5153
Long Island City, NY 11105, USA
Tel: (718) 721 4246
Fax: (718) 728 6108
e-mail: itsibts@aol.com
www.itsibts.com
Manufactured in the United States of America

ISBN 1-889720-08-9

For our son, Isma'il

Contents

A Fable

Once upon a time, long long ago, there was a little girl named Aziza. She lived in a small house in America and was very lonely because she had been forced to leave her far away home and had been made to come to America by her parents. She would sit alone often and remember her old home.

She missed the sun shine. The sun always shone in her far away home. Even when it rained, the sun was not far behind.

It was a place full of chico trees, her favorite fruit, and large green coconuts which had soft pulp and the tastiest of milk. There were elephants, giraffes, hyenas, and monkeys who ran on vast green plains. She missed all of these things, but most of all she missed the beautiful sea which had been behind her house.

Aziza would often stand for hours on end at her balcony and listen to the sea, hmmmm. The sea was so close she could smell its clear scent. She could walk to it and become mesmerized by the way the sun made the water sparkle like a million diamonds, rolling slowly and carelessly on the waves.

Her mother would always yell, "Be careful not to fall in!" And Aziza would not.

One day, when Aziza came home from school, her father made an announcement. "We're leaving for America!" he said. Aziza looked at her parents' faces, and they looked so happy.

"You'll see, " her mother told her, "that America is a beautiful place Aziza. You'll like it very much."

Aziza did not hear her mother. She ran to the kitchen and grabbed a chico, peeled it quickly and shoved it into her mouth. She tried to remember the taste because she knew she would never taste it again.

She ran to the balcony and looked at the sea one last time. She knew there would be no place in her bags to carry the sea. She knew she would never see it again. She knew she would never smell it again. She knew she would never touch it again.

She looked back at the pictures of the elephants she had drawn as a child. She did not dare run to the free range and look at the elephants because she knew, certainly, that she would cry. But her tears did not hear her thoughts because they began to well up in her eyes and slide down her face one by one then two by two, until there was a small steady stream running down both of her cheeks.

As the ship sailed off for America, Aziza watched the elephants, the chico trees, and coconut trees for the last time.

She looked out of the window of her cabin and watched the sea become the vast ocean and held the image in her eyes for as long as she could. She knew the sun would not shine as it did here anywhere else.

America was a strange place where people stared at her and called her frightful names. She spoke English very well and understood all the names that they called her. She could not understand why they called her these hurtful names.

But it was not her nature to rampage against people. She had a tender heart and had come from a beautiful place. She did not know how to be hurtful. Instead, she felt sorry for their ignorance and became sad.

So, Aziza read in her small room, in her small house, of fairy tale places, trying to recapture her home.

Every night she would pray to Allah to educated the ignorant. She would pray to Him to look over her mother and father, to look over her new home, but most of all she prayed that she would one day be able to return to her real home.

Unfortunately, the fairy tale world that she made up in her mind and the home she longed to return to were never to be. She learned slowly and surely that she would never be able to return home again.

She spent many moments with different circles of friends. She tried to find anyone who knew what a chico was. All of these so called friends eventually rejected her and called her names. She soon learned that she would not meet anyone who knew what a chico was. In time she became a loner, never trusting anyone. In her loneliness she sat in her room and wept.

She needed to find a place where elephants stood at peace looking at the sea and where chicos and coconuts grew in abundance. But where would she find such a place in America? Aziza realized she would have to design it herself.

She began to draw this place with crayons on sheets of paper. When the crayons became stubs, she thought of what else she could use to create her home.

With her saved allowance she purchased brushes of many sizes and a lots of tubes of bright colors. She brought a palate where she could mix the colors and create new ones. She brought many canvases of many sizes and took all of these things into her room.

Every evening after finishing her homework, Aziza spent many hours laboring over the many canvases.

She painted swirls, dots, and funny blotches. She used glue and pasted yarn, cloth, tree bark, leaves, anything she could find, to the canvas to bring texture to her visions.

One day, when she had them all finished, she lined up her paintings along the side of her room. Then, she stood back and looked at her canvases. She saw the glittering sea of diamonds; she saw the big chicos and the coconut trees. She saw her green plains, and when she walked closer, she felt she could even smell the sea.

Encouraged, she brought more canvases and began to paint again. After a while, her paintings spilled

out of her room and made their way into the hallway. Soon they lined the stairs and then they were everywhere.

They began to take up too much space in her small home.

"What do I do now?" she asked her parents.

Her mother encouraged her to bring her paintings to school and participate in the annual art show. Her father said he would be glad to drive her and help her put her paintings up.

Her parents said, "You should share your paintings with others. Then they can know about our home far away."

Aziza did not like that idea. "They will not understand my art," she said. "They are all mean. They do not even know what a chico is!" she screamed. And in her head she thought: "And they'll just come up with more names to hurt me."

Her parents calmed her down and said, "It is the job of those who have knowledge of new things to teach those who do not know."

Aziza thought about this. Then she realized that those people had not traveled and seen her home. They had no concept of the world which existed outside of their little space. She would show them her world. She would share it with them. With that being the case, Aziza entered the art show.

When the day for the art show came, Aziza was very nervous. She did not want the classmates to make fun of her art. It would hurt her deeply. She wanted to run and grab her paintings and take them into the car and have her father drive her home. Instead, she stood still. She waited beside her art work.

One by one her classmates stared with wonder and excitement at Aziza's work. Their parents began asking her mother and father where they had lived before. Everyone said that they had never seen such a bright place before.

One mother called it "heavenly."

Her paintings told them a tale of a far away place that they now wanted to visit and learn more about. Aziza was happy. They were speaking of her home and they understood its beauty.

She felt a nudge at her elbow, and she turned around. A girl from another class was standing there.

"Hey," she said and she pointed to one of the paintings. Aziza prepared herself for an insult.

"That's a chico, isn't it? I haven't had one in a really long time."

And Aziza did what she hadn't done in a really long time; she smiled.

Ibrahim's Search

One day a young boy named Ibrahim was listening to the Imam of his Masjid. He heard this Imam say that the Creator of everything and everyone was Allah.

At school the next day, Ibrahim said to his teacher, "Show me Allah. I want to see Him."

His teacher told Ibrahim that she could not produce Allah. Instead she leaned over to her book shelf and took out the Qur'an. She turned the pages and read to him some verses that proved Allah's existence.

She then turned to him and said, "Do you understand?" Now Ibrahim was only a young boy, and he didn't understand his teacher's point at all, so, as young boys do, he answered truthfully, "No, I don't understand."

"Well you see," the teacher began. And what followed next was a long lecture on how Allah is indeed everywhere and on how He created everything. But some of the big words she used confused him and when she had finished talking, Ibrahim did not understand any more than he did when she began talking.

The young boy was not thoroughly convinced by this proof and wanted real evidence.

So he looked at his teacher and said, "If you cannot show me Allah, I will ask someone who will."

After school he ran home. He walked into the yard and found his mother sitting on a bench. He threw his books down at her feet. His mother looked up, startled.

Ibrahim breathed very rapidly as he asked his mother, "Ummi," he asked, "can you show me Allah, please?"

His mother smiled and said, "I'm sorry Ibrahim, but I cannot do that. Allah cannot be seen by anyone. He has shown Himself through His Qur'an, His prophets, and this Earth's gifts to mankind."

"If I can't see Allah, how do I know that He's there?" he asked her.

"Every morning that you wake up, doesn't the sun rise?"

"Well I don't know if it rises, but it's bright when I wake up," he said with a smile.

"I'm being serious now, Ibrahim. And every evening the sun goes down and the night can be found. Allah allows the beautiful birds to sing for us, he allows the flowers to bloom for us. He makes the rivers run and the oceans glisten. He sends us rain for all the living things to grow. When you see these beautiful things in the world around you, you are seeing Allah's creations. No one else can do what Allah does. Allah is everywhere."

"I want to say thank you to Allah. And if He is everywhere, Ummi, may I go out to try and get a peek at Allah and thank Him personally?"

Ibrahim's mother smiled to herself and then said, "That's fine my son, for in Islam you are encouraged to ask questions and search for answers."

So that Saturday, with a small sack of food in hand, and a little bit of water, Ibrahim when on his search for his Creator.

After walking for a while, he saw a great mountain with many trees on it.   "Maybe," he said to himself, "that is Allah. Look at all the trees that guard against any enemies. Allah is truly strong."

As he walked along the outer edge of the mountain for a closer look, he noticed a stream going through the mountain and into the sea.

The boy wondered, "If this stream can go though the mountain, then surely this stream is stronger than the mountain."

He then looked at how the water flowed into the sea with great ease. "This stream is feeding the sea.

Surely the sea is greater than the stream, for the mountain is obeying the stream and the stream is obeying the sea."

He walked over to the sea and saw that it stretched very far. In fact, when he looked out at the sea he could see nothing else.

"Ah, this must be Allah," he tried to convince himself. "The water is everywhere, and Allah is everywhere, too! If I take some water, then I can keep Allah very close to me."

The young boy took out a small cup from his sack and filled it with water. He stared at it all morning long. He soon fell asleep, happy with his prize.

The sun was very high and bright. As the afternoon wore on, the sun became hotter and hotter. Soon, the water evaporated.

When Ibrahim woke up, he noticed that the water was gone.

"The sun must have taken the water," he thought. "Yes, of course. The sun must be Allah. It makes the plants grow. It can take up the water at will. The sun is definitely Allah." He tried to look at the sun, but it was too bright for him.

"I should have known. No Creator would want to be looked on by someone like me. That is why it is so far away. No matter. I will wait here until He tells me to move."

As the day passed on, the sun began to set in the horizon, and the moon appeared.

"The sun sets while the moon rises, but they do not crash into each other. How come?"

Ibrahim began to think even more. "Water is taken by the sun, but the seas never empty. Why? Water flows through a mountain, but the mountain does not crumble away. Why? There must be someone greater than all of these. Someone who holds everything together, but who?"

Ibrahim realized that he already knew the answer. His mouth opened up as he whispered "Allah," to himself.

For the first time he understood. His mother was right. It is Allah who holds all of this world together.

It's Allah that provides us with nature's beauty. It is Allah who allows the mountains to grow, the streams to run, the seas to exist, the birds to sing, the flowers to grow, the rain to fall, the people to live, the babies to smile. It is Allah alone who is the Almighty. It is He alone who is our Creator.

The Adventures of Sabse Oongli and Og

It happened again: the teasing, chasing, and hitting. A day hardly went by that Hasan wasn't made fun of: "*Sabse Oongli, Sabse Oongli, wears his kufi for his Ummi!*" *

Whether chanting through the school yard or whispering through the class, Hasan could not escape the teasing of the other students. And the reason behind all the trouble? Hasan tried to be a good Muslim.

---

* In the Urdu language, "sabse oongli" means "the best finger." Here, the meaning shows Hasan's love of making Salat. The "best finger" happens to be raised while sitting and saying the *Tashahud.*

During his classes he sat quietly while others giggled and played. He never disrespected his teachers or made fun of anyone. His homework was always neat, and he was ready to volunteer his help at a moment's notice.

What he liked to do most was call the adhan and do Salat. That's why the children called him *Sabse Oongli*.

Now, Hasan didn't much mind the *Sabse Oongli* meaning, but he didn't like the intention behind it. Everyone felt that he was trying to be a teacher's pet.

"Do you see the way he says please and thank you?" his classmates would say.

"Yeah, it's like he's in some contest or something," they would continue.

They would conclude, "Does he think he's better than us or what?"

On and on the students would say these things, behind his back or to his face. Nonetheless, Hasan never let what they said bother him.

It did hurt, but he would continue to behave the best he could by talking to and giving his *salaam* to those who were mean to him. This bothered them the most.

It was bad enough that Hasan was nice, but to be nice even when they were being mean was being too nice. They thought that this was the way Hasan was making fun of them. They thought he was getting a good laugh at their expense. They didn't understand that Hasan was just a nice person who could not be mean to anyone, even people who made fun of him.

They couldn't understand this because they were so mean, so cruel, they couldn't understand what being nice meant.

And most of all, they didn't understand what mattered to Hasan was what Allah thought, not what his classmates thought. Well, with Hasan being as weird as he was, the felt they'd seen it all. But, one day a new student arrived.

The new boy had a fiery temper, seldom spoke, and grunted a lot. It was because of these things that he received the name "Og" from his classmates. *

The school was preparing for its yearly sports competition against other schools. On Monday morning, after classes were over, there was a try-out for the track and field events.

"Assalam 'alaikum!" said the coach. "All right, everybody! I expect all those who want to participate in the try outs to be at the starting line! You have five minutes to get yourselves ready!" screamed the coach. "Now, when I call out your name, answer!" He began to call out the list of students.

One by one each student gave the common reply, "Here" or "Jee". However, when the coach called off the final name, what was heard was not a "Yes," a "Jee," or even a nod of the head.

A firm grunt had pushed its way towards the front of the crowd. All heads turned around and saw Og squatting on the floor with a scowl on his face. His huge body cemented itself into the playing field.

---

* In the Urdu language "og" means "fire."

20

"What was that?!" asked the coach with a tinge of surprise.

Again, *Og*'s grunt made its way over the heads of the other students and plopped itself in front of the coach.

Having searched and found the origin of the inhuman sound, the coach, staring at *Og*'s slumping body, asked, *"Is that boy okay?"*

"I guess that's his way of saying 'Yes,'" offered a student in the front row.

"Well, I hope he runs better than he speaks," commented the coach. With that said, the group of students got up and made their way to the starting blocks. The try-outs were about to begin.

As the students lined up to take their place, they noticed *Sabse Oongli* peeking out from the bleachers. He had always wanted to participate in sports but was too scared to. He was worried the other children would make fun of him and he was afraid he wouldn't be any good. His long thin body didn't look like the stuff athletes were made of.

Once they spotted Sabse Oongli, the other boys began to nudge each other. The whole group of thirty boys started staring at *Sabse Oongli*.

Soon, *Sabse Oonlgi* became aware that he was being looked at. He started sweating.

"Hey, I spy with my little eye something that looks scared," one boy said.

"Yeah, and I spy something with my little eye that's going to die!" cried another.

One by one, each boy started to pound their fist into their palm. Then, a chant started to rise from the mouths of all the boys: "Sabse Oongli, Sabse Oongli, wears his kufi for his Umi!" They slowly began to make their way towards the bleachers that protected Hasan.

"Sabse Oongli, Sabse Oongli, wears his kufi for his Ummi!" After hearing the cries ring out, the coach tried to stop the boys. Unfortunately, the boys were already running towards their prey.

"SABSE OONGLI, SABSE OONGLI, WEARS HIS KUFI FOR HIS UMMI!" Like a pack

of wild dogs all thirty boys rushed at poor little *Sabse Oongli.*

Paralyzed by fear for a few seconds, *Sabse Oongli* saw his doom racing to get him. He couldn't even move his feet or legs to move. He heard his heart beat mixing with the cries of hatred from the boys.

Then, somewhere deep inside his heart, he got the courage to move his legs. It was a little hard at first, but he slowly began to run.

The boys, seeing their victim try to make his escape, charged even faster.

Sabse Oongli knew at this moment that he was not going to allow himself to be injured again. He was tired of the humiliation. Though he couldn't take on all thirty boys, he could make their time trying to catch him as difficult as possible.

The boys swarmed the bleachers like hungry rats. At the sound of their feet stampeding the wooden boards, *Sabse Oongli* ran faster than he (or any other student in that school's history) had ever run. His long body sliced through the air at top speed. He jumped onto the field and started running along the track because he knew a wide open space was better for spped. The crowd of raging boys tailed along behind him around the track.

By this time the coach had called out some other teachers for help. When the staff arrived at the field, they saw little Hasan racing yards ahead of a frustrated and tired looking group of boys.

One boy called out with a gasp, "Let's go! We can't let him get away!"

"I can't believe he's running so fast!" cried another as he brushed a gallon of sweat off his nose..

One by one the boys began to fall to the side of the track. They couldn't keep up with Hasan's speed and pace. The teachers were shocked at the sight.

Some of the school's best runners were lying on the ground gasping for air while Hasan barely looked winded.

Sabse Oongli finally rounded the last curve and made his way towards the teachers. At the same time many of the other boys were barely stumbling or crawling towards them.

"You...you're...you're just lucky," said one student.

"Now listen," started the coach, "I know that you people may not like Hasan that much, but you are all still Muslim brothers, and you'd better start behaving like it. Do you understand me?"

Some of the boys just rolled their eyes. They had heard this speech before.

"I mean it. I don't want to see any more problems," repeated the coach.

"I don't think they are going to change much," said *Sabse Oongli.*

"I guess we need to convince them in some way. You know, ease them into it," said the coach.

Suddenly, everyone there heard a rhythmic breathing make its way towards Hasan. The group of boys parted, leaving a path for the one they named *Og*

He had seen it all. He had seen the anger in the eyes of the boys. He had seen Hasan run for his life. Yes, he had seen Hasan prove himself.

Og placed himself between the other boys and Hasan. He then put his arms up to his chest and faced the crowd of boys. He bared his teeth and let out a firm grunt. With that said, the other boys understood clearly what *Og* was saying. *"Stay away or you'll get pounded."*

"Are you sure that boy's okay?" asked the coach while scratching his head.

The school's track and field competition came and went. *Sabse Oongli* and *Og* raced on the same relay team and won. They would go on to share many adventures together in the years to come.

As for the boys, a lot of them soon began to learn that trying to be a good Muslim wasn't a weakness but a strength that you carried with you on your real and most important race- the race towards Allah.

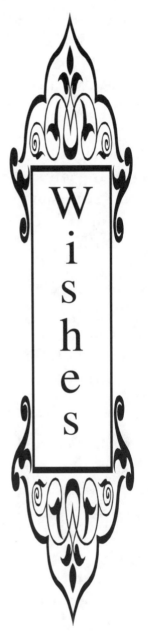

Wishes

Once there was a musician who worked very hard at trying to compose a melody. A melody that would make the birds jealous. So, each day he would go out into the woods and sit.

Pleasant melodies would wander through his mind, yet he could never stop a melody long enough to capture it and pass it along to his fingers. He could never play it.

As he sat each morning, he disturbed one particular forest-dwelling jinn. Each day the jinn had to put up wuth the sounds that came out of the musician's badly-tuned guitar. Until one day, the jinn could no longer stand it.

This jinn tore out of his home and rushed quickly to the musician. He snatched up the musician's guitar and said, "If you will stop playing this guitar in my home," the jinn opened his arms wide gesturing to the entire woods, "I will grant you three wishes."

The musician was startled at the sight of the jinn. The jinn was of such height and unusual appearance. The musician had never seen such a creature. The musician gasped in terror before he realized what the jinn of the woods had offered him.

"Oh," the musician closed his eyes and thought, "three wishes. I must choose my wishes wisely. First, I would wish for a magnificent guitar. The best in the world."

As the musician opened his eyes, before him lay the magnificent guitar. Its body was made of opal, and it was trimmed with gold.

The musician greedily picked up the guitar and tried to play it.

This guitar, the most magnificent guitar in the entire world, made the same sound as his old guitar.

"Why- you have tricked me!" the musician said to the wood jinn.

The jinn replied, "You only asked for a guitar. You didn't ask for the ability to play it."

"Ah," the musician smiled, "I didn't choose wisely enough. I wish I could play this guitar: the most magnificent guitar in the world." He picked up the guitar once more and began to play.

A wondrous melody issued from the guitar. The musician thought to himself, "Oh, how wisely I have chosen the second wish."

It made the musician feel great.

The birds flew around him, captured by the melody. The trees shook with the beauty of melody.

The wind began to flow in rhythm to the melody. The

melody became more and more intense as the musician played.

As the wind became harsh, the musician became afraid and tried to stop playing, but he could not.

He had asked for the ability to play. He had not, however, asked for the ability to stop playing.

Soon, all of nature was responding to the wondrous melody. Thunder began to sound; mountains began to shift; the earth began to tremble; the birds began to screech, and the trees began to fall.

The musician became very frightened, yet his fingers would not stop. They moved swiftly like a spider. He could not control them.

His heart beating fast, in fear of his own life, the musician finally screamed, "I WISH IT WOULD ALL GO AWAY!!"

The melody ceased slowly. When it was finished, nothing could be heard. The wind was no more; the birds were no more; the trees were no more; the thunder was no more; the mountains were no more; the earth was no more. The musician sat alone in total darkness...

He had not chosen the last wish wisely.

Finders
Keepers

Harun had looked forward to his first day at his new Muslim school. His mom and dad had prepared him a few weeks before by explaining to him the behavior and work that will be expected of him in his classes.

Although Harun was only six years old and going to the first grade, his parents wanted him to understand the importance of education.

Then again, he was only six, so the only thing that Harun could really remember about his parents' speeches was: "Remember, always be a good Muslim."

The day soon came when Harun would put this message to good use. During recess, Harun found a twenty dollar bill on the floor near the front door of the school.

Harun looked around but could not seem to find anyone who might own the money.

He slowly bent down and picked up the stray bill. To a six year old boy a twenty dollar bill is almost as much as a million dollars.

It was because of this that he understood the importance of having to give this money back to the person that it belonged to.

That afternoon, he decided to ask some of his classmates what he should do with the money. Since he practically knew everyone at the school, he chose to speak to three different people to see what kind of opinion he would get. He decided to first ask Adnan for his opinion.

At first, Adnan didn't much care about the fact that Harun had even found the money. What

concerned him more were the things that could be bought with it.

"Wow! We could like buy a lot of candy with all of this money!" said Adnan.

"I know, but shouldn't we try to find out who owns it? Maybe that person wants to buy candy, too."

"Aw, naw. If that person wanted candy, they wouldn't have thrown away the money."

"How do you know the person threw it away?"

"Why else would someone give up twenty dollars? So, what are we going to buy with this money? I mean we could get fifty bags of potato chips, new gym shoes and....."

Harun left Adnan standing there by the see-saws dreaming about all of the candy that he was talking about.

Harun then walked towards Afifah. She seemed like she would give him better advice. After all, she was the class monitor.

When Afifah saw Harun walking toward her with the money in his hand, she immediately said to him, "Where did you steal that money from?"

Harun was shocked. "I didn't steal any money. I found this money by the door. I wanted to know if you could help me find the person who lost this or at least help me ......"

"Hide your crime? I don't think so. I will not be an accomplice to your game of lies."

Afifah was really into watching cop shows. She always managed to confuse the students and her teacher with her style of speaking.

As such, Harun stood there confused. Shaking his head, Harun responded, "Huh?"

"You clearly took that money. How else could you have come across that much money?" she said, squinting her eyes into thin lines under her Hijab.

"But...but...I didn't do anything. I figured that since you are the class monitor you can..."

"Aid you in a quick escape from the scene of the crime? I don't think so."

Harun saw that the conversation was going nowhere, so he left Afifah, who was yelling out, "Young brother, don't go onto the wrong side of the tracks! You need Allah! Read your Qur'an my young brother! Iqra!"

While her voice was slowly trailing off, Harun made his way towards Jahur, who was busy trying to build a house out of the other students' shoes.

"Um, Jahur. Are you busy?"

In a very slow voice, Jahur responded, "I almost have it, but you can talk if you want."

"Okay. I found a twenty dollar bill, and I'm not sure what to do. Part of me wants to keep it, and another part of me wants to give it back. What do you think I should do?"

With sweat dripping from his forehead onto a pair of sneakers, Jahur said, "Put...it...back."

Harun was slightly confused. "What do you mean 'Put it back'?"

"Well, why should you worry about this money? Just put it back and let someone else worry about it. Let that bill be someone else's problem." With that said, Jahur went to wipe his brow with a shoe lace.

Lunch time was coming to an end, and Harun thought about what everyone had said. If he spent the money, it would be unfair to the person who lost it. If he just put it back, some other person might not have the intention of giving it back.

Harun then remembered what his parents had told him about being a good Muslim.

It was then that he decided to give the money to his teacher, Sr. Nejla.

When he explained what had happened, Sr. Nejla said, "I'm so glad that you gave me the money. One of the parents had lost it after dropping off their child. I told her that she shouldn't worry about the money being stolen. We have very nice students in this class, Alhumdulillah.

Harun felt very happy with himself. As a reward for his honesty, Sr. Nejla gave him a "good student" award.

Mommie, Mommie... There's a lie in My stomach!

Khalid never really concerned himself with his grades. He knew they probably weren't all that important in the long run. He really couldn't worry about things like getting high marks. A grade didn't really reflect how smart he was, it just couldn't. So what if he didn't study or his teacher thought he didn't pay enough attention in class!

He knew he was smart, he knew that he could read books when he was ready, and he knew he didn't need to listen in class because his teachers were really, reaallly, realllllyyyyyy borrrrriiiinnnngggg.

 Right now, right this very minute, though, he worried about how things looked on the test in front of him. He absorbed himself with correcting the signature on the page with *white out.*

Unfortunately, that just didn't work very well. The *white out* did not match the page. Who knew there were so many shades of white? He decided to start all over again and began by scraping off the *white out.* When using the side of a nickel didn't work, he began to use his father's sandpaper.

Little by little the test paper started looking like a big mess. A small hole began to grow around the thin space which he had rubbed at. As a last resource, Khalid glued the ends of the hole together and painted the blotches using some white spray paint. He looked at it critically. Well, it would have to do.

By this time it was already late. Khalid was very tired and just wanted to go to sleep. He wrote his father's name the best he could and fell asleep.

The next day when the teacher asked for everyone to hand up their signed tests, Khalid pulled out his test paper very carefully. Since he was the first person in the row, Khalid placed his test paper at the bottom of his row's pile, hoping that the teacher wouldn't pay too much attention to it, or better yet, skip over it.

He looked on as the teacher was checking all of the test's signatures, he carefully watched her face for any expressions. If her face stayed the same, it would mean that she did not find his phony signature. If her face began to frown, it would mean that he was caught.

Khalid held his breath. Test after test her face did not change. After all of the tests were checked, the teacher began to start her new lesson.

Khalid smiled and in his head he said: "Yeeessss." He had succeeded. Sr. Hanan did not catch him. He released his breath and let out a silent: "Heh, heh, heh."

"This was too easy," he said to himself.

"If I can do this to Sr. Hanan, I can probably do this in every other class. I won't ever have to study again!" he screamed out loud in his mind.

As he left class he said, really loudly, "See you in homeroom, Sr. Hanan!"

She just looked up from her desk and said, "Inshallah."

Throughout the entire day, in the lunchroom, in the gymnasium and in all of his classes, Khalid wore a bright smile on his face. He had learned the secret. The way to get through life successfully was to cheat.

After this morning's incident, he knew he was good at it. Or so he thought.

When the last bell of the day rang, the entire homeroom class went quickly towards the door. Khalid, on the other hand, took his time. He did not want this very successful day to end too quickly. He collected

his books quietly and slowly began to slide his way out the door with his bright smile still intact. Then, it happened.

"Oh, Khalid. Can you please come here for a minute?" asked Sr. Hanan.

Khalid stopped dead in his tracks. His heart began to speed up in its beating.

"What could she possibly want?" he wondered to himself.

Surely she had not caught his act. This morning she passed by his test, her face didn't change at all, and she hadn't said anything to him.

Khalid slowly turned around and walked towards her. He could feel the sweat begin to form on the back of his neck and under his shirt.

"Yes, Sr. Hanan," he said in a whisper.

"I wanted to ask you if you've chosen your project for the science fair," she said.

"Whew," he thought, "I was worried for nothing. I better stop sweating and play this off smoothly."

He said, "Um, yes, I have. It's going to be about the solar system," he replied, his voice a bit too high.

She continued to talk to him about the project, but all he could think about was how he was safe again.

By the end of her questioning, he had on his bright smile again.

As he headed out the door again, Sr. Hanan called out, "Oh, by the way...."

Still smiling, Khalid turned quickly and sang out, "Yes, Sr. Hanan."

"Who's signature is on this test paper?"

His mouth visibly dropped. He was busted.

"Are you all right?" she asked.

Khalid's mouth was still open. How did she find out?

"Wha...wha...what do you mean?" he stuttered.

"Well, your test has a big hole in it with splotches of white spray paint and *white out* all over it where the signature is. What was I supposed to think?"

"Um...um...um, I...I...I...um...I. Well, what happened is that...um...my...my...my sister was sitting at the dinner table where I had laid out my test paper at my father's spot, at the head of the table," Khalid turned to look out the window for a moment, to get his story straight.

"Yes, Khalid? And then what happened?" Sr. Hanan interrupted his idea.

"And um, she uuum, spilled some of her juice on it. You know just a drop. And I knew my father would get really mad, he gets really mad, really, really mad if anyone sits at his spot at the dinner table. And, naturally, I didn't want my sister, she's my little sister, to get into trouble or anything.

"So I grabbed a table napkin to wipe it off, and I rubbed too hard, and the paper got a hole in it and then it was really a bad scene because how could my father sign the paper now? So, I had to fix the paper so my sister, my little sister, would not get into trouble. So, I had to use *white out* and other stuff so the paper would look like new again because if my father asked what had happened, well then," he began to slow down and looked into Sr. Hanan's eyes, "then, it would be really bad for my little sister," he paused.

"So you see, I did it to save my sister from getting yelled at from my father, who, did I mention, can get really angry if he wants to." And in his mind he said, "That ought to do it because it sounds right to me." Then he smiled.

"That doesn't explain, Khalid, why this signature looks like yours."

Khalid frowned. He had to think quickly. "Oh, did I forget that part? See. After the hole and the *white out* and all the other stuff, I still couldn't fix the paper, so I brought it to my mother and asked her if I could sign for my father, so he wouldn't get mad at my little sister. And she said O.K."

"Why didn't your mother sign it?"

"My mother," Khalid thought for a moment. He looked up at the ceiling. "Oh," he looked down very quickly. "She can't read," he whispered.

Upon hearing this Sr. Hanan did not pursue the matter. She did not want to humiliate Khalid or his mother. She knew there were some women who were never given the opportunity to learn how to read.

Sr. Hanan just stared at him. She wasn't upset about the fact that he signed his father's signature, she understood that he must have felt humiliated about having to show his parents a bad grade, but she was disappointed that he lied.

She was also disappointed that he neither shared the grade with his father, nor had he read it for his illiterate mother.

"Khalid why couldn't you just show your parents your grade?"

"I just told you what happened, Sister Hanan."

"Yes I know Khalid, even though your father would get very upset, and I don't want to suggest that you provoke his anger, you should have at least tried to read your grade aloud to your mother. I'm sure she would have understood and maybe she could have told your father for you. I don't agree with not discussing the grade with them. I believe I will have to phone your home tonight and share the grade with your parents."

"Okay," Khalid said as he made a plan to race home.

He reached his front door panting. When he went into the living room, he found his mother reading a hadith text.

"Assalam 'alaikum, what's the rush?" his mother asked.

"Oh, mom, I'm waiting for a call from the coach of the track team. He thinks he might let me try out this year. So, I'm really excited."

"That's wonderful, Khalid! I know how much that means to . . . "

Khalid didn't even hear his mother, though, as he raced past her, plopped his books in the hall, and sat himself on a stool, right under the kitchen phone.

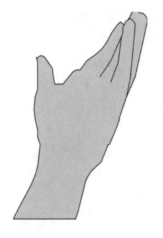

He waited and waited. His father was almost done preparing dinner, his mother began to set the table, and his little sister came down to help.

"So what's this phone vigil?" his father whispered to his mother.

"The track coach is going to call. I guess the team means a lot to him," his mother whispered back.

"Oh," his father smiled.

At last the phone rang. "Yes," Khalid said into the receiver.

'Assalam 'alaikum, Khalid. Are your parents home?" asked his teacher.

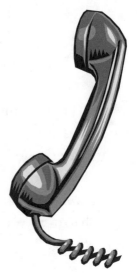

Khalid pointed to himself when he saw his parents looking at him, and he made his way around the corner into the hall.

"Oh, Sister Hanan. I'm sorry; they aren't here. They won't be home until really late. So, I guess you can't speak with them today, but I'll tell them you called okay, bye," and he quickly hung up the phone.

"Whew," he said and smiled. This lying thing was a cinch." He was the master liar, and he knew how to make it work for him.

"Oh, you look happy," his mother said. "Good news, huh?"

"Yeah, Ummi, good news," Khalid said as he heaped a huge helping of everything onto his plate.

That night, before he went to bed, his little sister knocked on his door. "What do you want Aliyah?" he grunted.

Aliyah, who was indeed his little sister, leaned in the door way and said, "I just want to ask you something."

"What do you want? Hurry up, 'Cause I'm tired."

"Well, yesterday I saw you trying to hide your test paper and then I saw you write daddy's name on it. You didn't see me, but I was right there."

"I didn't do that!"

"Yes, you did. I saw you, but I won't tell. I just want to know how you did it."

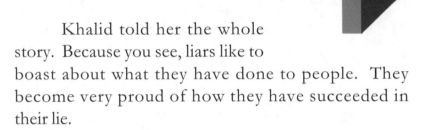

Khalid told her the whole story. Because you see, liars like to boast about what they have done to people. They become very proud of how they have succeeded in their lie.

Khalid ended the story with, "So you see...I've got it made because whenever Sister Hanan calls, I'll tell her Umi and Daddy aren't home.

And if she writes letters, I'll get them first and then tear them up."

Aliyah listened to the whole story and then her small eyes opened up a little. She said, "You know, you're going to be really busy with all that stuff. You won't have time to do anything else. Because see, once you tell one lie you have to go on telling others to cover all of your first lies. So really when you tell one lie, you have to lie another time to cover up the first one, then lie again to cover the other two, then. . . . "

Khalid interrupted Aliyah and smiled widely, "Of course I can do all of that, because I am the master liar."

Aliyah's eyes opened up very wide and she said, "Tell me one thing Khalid because I really need to know. This thing will convince me you are the master liar, okay.?"

"What? " he asked boastfully- his hands behind his head, his chair leaning back a bit.

"How did you fool Allah?"

Khalid's mouth fell open, and his stomach twisted into a big knot, like a wet towel being wrung out. He doubled over and fell to the floor when he realized his lie could only fool people, and not Allah.

He became all hot and sweaty. Then, he shivered, and he kept on shivering.

His parents ran up to help him. He was sick-

sick all night long. His parents didn't know what was wrong.

In the morning, he said he just had too much to eat and that he was going to school anyway. His mother asked if he was truly okay. He said, "Yeah" and ran out. He couldn't even look at her.

He had to figure out what he was going to do. He spent most of the morning in deep thought.   He knew he hadn't fooled Allah, and he didn't know what to do.

During third period, he received a note to go to Sr. Hanan's room. "Oh brother, now all I need is for her to give me a note," he thought.

When he got there, he saw her writing at her desk. "I'll just throw the note away," he thought.

Just then the door opened up behind him and in walked his mother and father. Khalid turned purple, and he began to sweat.

"Khalid, we were really worried about you this morning, so we're here to take you home," his mother began. She proceeded to put her hadith book into her purse.

Sr. Hanan looked at her and said, "Oh, I didn't know you could read?"

His mother looked at Sister Hanan, and it was then that it all fell apart. Khalid knew he didn't fool Allah and that it finally came back to him. And now he would have to begin his apologies to his parents and Sr. Hanan. Then he would have to apologize to Allah, and he knew that it wasn't going to be an easy day for him.

"No Hablo
Español"

It all started when his father found a Muslim
school in which to enroll Isma'il. The idea of attending
a full-time Muslim school really appealed to Isma'il. He
had been learning about Islam at home from his father
and mother and looked forward to sharing his
experiences with other children his age.

But when Isma'il arrived for his fist day of classes,
some students at the school took one look at him and
didn't expect him to know anything about Islam. They
figured that if people weren't from Pakistan or an Arab
country, they weren't really Muslims.

Although Isma'il could be confused for being
Greek, Italian, Brazilian, or even French, he had the
distinct appearance of being Hispanic. It didn't really
matter which Spanish country he came from. As far
as the students were concerned, it was all the same.

Now, kids can be cruel. Every time Isma'il would try to get involved in a conversation with some of the students, they would always laugh and respond: "No hablo *Español*." "I don't speak Spanish." At first Isma'il thought that he had an accent, and the students weren't really able to understand him.

"I can speak English," he would naively respond.

But the students would just laugh and stare at him saying, "No hablo *Español*."

After a few weeks of trying to explain to the children that he was able to talk to them, he gave up trying to say anything and just stayed quiet in school.

Whether he was in class, at lunch, or in gym, Isma'il would not open his mouth to respond to anyone, even to the teachers.

Because he never spoke in class, the teachers thought that he couldn't speak English. The other students encouraged such thoughts by saying that Isma'il had just come from some Spanish country and was unable to speak the language.

The teachers found this rather difficult to understand considering that Isma'il consistently scored very good grades on all his tests and homework. So, even though he never said anything in class, he was a very good student when it came to all of his subjects.

Realizing this, some students suggested that Isma'il was probably cheating from other students.

Not quite believing such a suggestion, the teachers decided to have a meeting about the new student who did not speak.

Ideas were passed around the table that ranged from Isma'il being a deaf genius to him taking a vow of silence. One teacher finally decided to have someone get Isma'il and send him in so they could somehow ask him what the problem was.

Isma'il sat there at the end of a long table staring at all of his teachers. The question was then asked: "Isma'il, why don't you speak in class?"

He sat there for a moment. He wondered if he should tell them or not. Would they not be able to understand him also? Would they laugh at him?

After taking a deep breath Isma'il said, "I choose not speak because the students in this school have told me that they don't understand me when I speak."

His words never sounded more clear. They seemed to vibrate off the faces of those who were in front of him.

He waited anxiously for a response.

"Isma'il, you speak very well, Alhumdulillah. Unfortunately, some of our students do not behave very kindly. They were playing a joke on you."

"A very cruel joke," added another teacher.

Isma'il sat there very quietly. Then he asked, "Why would they want to do something like that for?"

"Well, Isma'il. Although Islam teaches us that every Muslim should be treated with respect, many of our students and their families haven't met many Muslims that come from different cultures," said his Arabic teacher.

His math teacher added, "It's important for you to realize that the fault is not with you but with the other students. They need to be shown that someone from another background is still a Muslim. Not every Muslim speaks only Urdu or Arabic."

They all decided to show the students that things weren't always predictable.

Every day, just before Zuhr Salat, a student was asked to call the adhan. Some of the students got scared at the thought of calling it because they were nervous about how their voices might sound.

On this particular day the teacher had asked Isma'il to call the Adhan, or call to prayer. Many of the students looked at each other and started to laugh to themselves.

This, however, did not keep Isma'il from walking toward the Masjid, because he remembered the encouragement the teachers had given him.

Isma'il took a deep breath and let his voice flow from his mouth like the wind. His voice reverberated across the walls, sounded outside of the Masjid windows, and echoed all through the huge halls. Allah had gifted Isma'il with a beautiful voice.

All of the students sat dumbfounded, with their mouths open.

One child leaned into another and said, "He's Spanish. How can he speak Arabic so well?" The other student shrugged his shoulders.

There was a man who was in the back of the Masjid. Sitting quietly, waiting, and listening to the sound which was emanating from Ismail's mouth. The man's eyes were closed, and he was smiling.

He was pleased to know that such a young child was able to utter the words of the adhan so clearly and with such wonderful recitation.

After Isma'il finished the Adhan, he went to his spot on the Masjid floor and sat down, alone.

One of the boys from his class turned to him and winked his eye.

"That was beautiful," Daud mouthed.

The boy sitting next to him elbowed Daud to shut up and not to talk to Isma'il. Daud looked at the boy, got up, and sat next to Isma'il.

Daud's parents had always taught him that Allah made Muslims in every color and shape, from every country and culture. And now finally, Daud had the courage to put that knowledge into action.

Isma'il smiled a bit when Daud sat next to him. After Salat was over, the man who was sitting in the back row walked up to Isma'il. He laid a hand on his shoulder and said, "Assalam alaikum my son. I listened to your adhan today and was very impressed. It's wonderful for me to hear our young Muslim men learn the beautiful words of the adhan and utter them so wonderfully."

"Jazakallah ul khair," said Isma'il.

"Mi hijo, yo quiero visitar sus padres un dia. Quiero decirles que ellos tienen un hijo bueno que esta aprendiendo la fe de Islam en una manera maravillosa." *

Isma'il was stunned. How could another Muslim speak Spanish so well. Isma'il thought only his family were Spanish Muslims. Daud slapped Isma'il on the back when the man had gone.

"Do you know who that was?" he asked Isma'il.

"No, who was that?"

"That was the Imam of the big Masjid in the city. He was trained at Al-Azhar and he was among the top of his class. He's a great scholar."

"And he was Hispanic?"

"Yeah. And of course he has the entire Qur'an

---

* "My son, I would like to visit your parents one day. I would like to tell them that they have a good child that is learning the Islamic faith marvelously."

memorized. He also has one of the most beautiful voices of any Imam I have heard. And," Daud looked straight into Isma'il's face, "He's one of the most intelligent people I have had the pleasure to meet," and with that Daud laughed.

Isma'il smiled.

"Hey, how about coming to my house for dinner some day? Huh?" Daud asked.

"Insha'llah, I would be really happy to," and this time, Isma'il's smile reached all across his face and he laughed.

It took several more days, but soon, with the help of the teachers and lessons from the Qur'an, eventually the children recognized that Islam was the religion for, and of, all people. So, day by day, a change came about in the students, and soon Isma'il had many friends.

There were still those who continued to taunt him, and he knew he would always encounter those people. But this time he had friends who said, "Ahhhhh, don't listen to them. They're just jealous of your voice," or "They don't know what they're talking about. Don't waste your time on them."

Eventually, the teachers told the students that when a Muslim made fun of or was prejudice against another, he or she would have to answer to Allah on the day of judgment, and no one wanted that.

"And among His signs is a creation of the heavens and earth, and the difference of your languages and colors. Verily, in that are indeed signs for men of sound knowledge."
(Qur'an 30:22)

Playground Sounds

"What do we say when we're thinking of
Allah?"
"What do we say when we're thinking of
Allah?"
When starting anything:
"Bismillah"
Like getting on a swing:
"Bismillah"
When having an intention: "Inshallah"
Like meeting with a good friend: "Inshallah"
To show appreciation:
"Mashallah"
for your teacher's education:
"Mashallah"
When you want to praise: "Subhaanallah"
Allah's sunny days:
"Subhaanallah"
If you sneeze: "Alhamdulillah"
You must say one of these: "Alhamdulillah"
And if you do something wrong:
"Astaghferullah"
You'll just try to be strong:
"Inshallah!"

Do you Kung-Fu?

Every weekend Zainab would watch her brother walk out the house with his sports bag in hand, leaving for his martial arts class.

She would look out of the window as he made his way towards his bicycle in the garage. While he was pedaling away, she would always ask the same question to her mother, "Mom, why can't I go with Khabir to his classes?"

Her mother would in turn give the same answer that she

began to give since the question first made its appearance, "You are too young to take that Kunratee or Kane-fu that Khabir is learning. Besides, it's not very lady like to fight."

Zainab would automatically respond, "But mom, I'm nine years old!" Unfortunately, these words fell on deaf ears. She knew better than continue the discussion, so as usual, she'd just walk away.

It was the last sentence her mother said, however, that always seemed strange to Zainab. She just couldn't understand why it was wrong for a girl to learn how to fight.

She knew that getting into fights or picking on someone that was weaker than her was wrong, but what was the problem with learning to defend yourself? Why couldn't girls practice martial arts forms and do exercises to strengthen themselves?

Zainab was so desperate about learning the martial arts that she would come up with ways of learning some moves from her brother.

At first she would try to watch him work out in the garage with the punching bag, but she would get tired because he would do stretching exercises for about an hour.

"Oh, this will never do. There has to be another way."

She figured that if she attacked her brother occasionally, he would have to defend himself. She would then be able to see what he was being taught at his school.

When the day came that Khabir had to leave for his classes, Zainab stood behind the closet door.

As her brother was walking by the ajar door, she leaped out at him, letting out a horrible scream.

"AAAHHH-YYYEEEYYAAA!"

Instinctively, Khabir caught her flying arms in mid-air and flung her onto the nearby couch. Not to be out done, Zainab re-grouped herself and threw her whole body, pillows in hand, at her brother again.

"AAAHHH-YYYYEEEYYAAA!"

Again, Khabir caught her mid-air and carefully flung her to the other side of the living room. She lay on the floor sandwiched between the two pillows.

"What is going on in here!" yelled her mother. "Khabir, are you trying to kill your sister or something! I told you not to practice that Kung-Du..Moo-shoo thing in the living room."

"Mom! I didn't do anything."

"So, I suppose your sister threw herself across the room and squished her head between two pillows on purpose, right?"

"But I didn't start anything. She came and attacked me. I mean...all I was doing was walking along the hallway, and "BAM!" Zai comes flying out of nowhere, pillows in hand. What was I supposed to do, get hit in the face with two fluffy pillows?"

"Yes!"

"Mom, you're kidding me!"

Zainab slowly rolled off her back and softly added, "Mom, Khabir's telling the truth. I did try to attack him."

Zainab's mother looked at her and then turned to her bother. "I'm sure you had a good reason. Your brother can get quite crafty at times."

"But mom..."

"Don't take that tone of voice with me young man!"

"I can't believe this! How come you're always taking her side?"

"Hush." Turning towards her daughter she continues, "Now, go on dear. What's the problem?"

"Well, I was kinda hoping that he could teach me some Kung-fu."

"I thought I told you that you weren't going to learn any of that Kung-du stuff."

"It's Kung- Fu, mom!" Khabir quickly added.

"Well, it's all the same to me. What I do know is this, I do not want you to learn how to fight."

"But, mom. I don't understand why," said Zainab, who looked up at her mother.

Her mother looked at her daughter and responded, "Well, I just don't think it's right for a girl your age to fight or even be interested in fighting. It's just so unlady-like. Imagine, you wearing a Hijab in a class full of boys, throwing punches and kicks. Leave all the fighting to the boys. You shouldn't have to worry about those things."

Zainab just sat there. She knew it would take a lot to convince her mother to see things from her point of view.

Khabir took a look at the time and realized that he had to go. "Mom, I have to go now. Insha'llah, I'll be back at the usual time."

"Take care. Assalamu 'alaikum," said his mother, and she made her way back to the den.

"Wa 'alaikum assalam," he responded.

Before he left, however, he whispered a strange message to Zainab: "Third case, second shelf, Wing Chun." Then, he left.

She wasn't quiet sure what that meant. After some time she realized that he was probably talking about the bookshelves in his bedroom.

She slowly made her way up to his room, found the correct case, the right shelf and the strange titled book.

She looked at the cover of the book, then opened it and began to read the introduction:

With the reading of these words, a smile came upon Zainab's face. "So, my idea of wanting to fight isn't such a strange one," she thought to herself.

She continued to read about these famous female fighters.

Zainab read on for hours. She had never heard of such strong women before.

"I wonder if there are such women in Islamic history," she thought to herself.

As if on cue, Zainab glanced her eyes on a footnote that her brother had written on the back cover. It referred to someone name Khalwah. Zainab read on and found out that Khalwah was the sister of a Muslim general who encouraged her fellow sisters, who were armed with tent poles, to fight against the Byzantine army.

Women warriors were common during certain times in history.

They engaged in various forms of defense, such as archery, sword fighting, and hand to hand combat.

One of the most famous warriors was a woman by the name of Wing Chun

It was this newly found information that gave Zainab the strength to speak to her mother one more time.

"Oh, mother," she called out.

"Yes, dear. What is it?"

For the next half hour Zainab shared with her mother what she had learned about Khawlah. Slowly but surely her mother began to hear her daughter's point of view.

"So, you see, I'd just be carrying on the line of strong Muslim women."

With some hesitation her mother responded, "Okay, I understand your point. You can learn this Kung Fu Shoo thing but under one condition. Your brother will teach you himself."

Hugging her mother tightly, Zainab replied, "No problem, mom. Thank you very much."

"Well, let's see what your brother says."

When asked, Khabir agreed. Although the workouts and training were very difficult, Zainab became a very good fighter. She even beat Khabir a few times.

In years to come, she would teach other young Muslim sisters the art of Kung-Fu. In no time at all many sisters were teaching other Muslim girls the physical part of becoming Islamic women warriors.

Selected Titles Available From IBTS

Ahmad Deen and the Jinn at Shaolin
By Yahiya Emerick

A once in a lifetime chance! Ahmad Deen is one of ten lucky students in his school who gets an all-expense paid trip to China. But instead of getting a history lesson, Ahmad may become a victim *of history* as he is thrust in the middle of a bizarre web of superstition, corruption and ancient hatreds that seek to destroy all who interfere.

Who kidnapped his room-mate? What clue can only be found in the Shaolin Temple? How will Ahmad learn the Kung-Fu skills he'll need to defeat the powers of darkness. or will he fall prey to the mysterious *Jinn at Shaolin?* Illustrated, 120 pages.

The Army of Lions
By Qasim Najar

Get ready for swashbuckling and deeds of valor at its finest! The Army of Lions is coming! Take yourself back to the days when a believer and his faith could destroy every evil tyrant, when the brave and true could sweep over the plains and cities of the world and make them take notice. If you're impressed by unswerving determination and faith that conquers all, then be prepared to join the Army of Lions! A full length fiction novel set in the golden age of Islam. Illustrated, 176 pages.

Layla Deen and the Case of the Ramadan Rogue
By Yahiya Emerick

Somebody's trying to ruin her Ramadan! Layla Deen and her family were just settling in to break a long days fast when their mother came running from the kitchen and cried, *"Someone stole the food for Iftar!"* Layla knew it was a terrible crime and decided to get to the bottom of this mystery. See what happens! Illustrated. 54 pages.

Isabella: A Girl of Muslim Spain
By Yahiya Emerick

A classic tale about a young girl who finds Islam, and danger, amidst the harrowing religious conflicts of medieval Muslim Spain.

Experience firsthand what life was like in the splendid Muslim city of Cordoba. See through the eyes of Isabella as she struggles with her father's Christian beliefs and finds that life is not always as easy as people think. Embark on a journey into history, into the heart, as you follow her path from darkness into light.

Highly recommended for teenagers and young adults. A sensitive and realistic portrayal from a unique point of view unlike anything you have ever read. Illustrated, 120 pages.

Ahmad Deen and the Curse of the Aztec Warrior
By Yahiya Emerick

Where is he? Ahmad Deen and his sister Layla thought they were getting a nice vacation in tropical Mexico. But what they're really going to get is a hair-raising race against time to save their father from becoming the next victim of an ancient, bloody ritual!

How can Ahmad save his father *and* deal with his bratty sister at the same time? To make matters worse, no one seems to want to help them find the mysterious lost city that may hold the key to their father's whereabouts. And then there's that jungle guide with the strangely familiar jacket. Are they brave enough—or crazy enough, to take on the *Curse of the Aztec Warrior?* Illustrated, 60 pages.

Learning About Islam
By Yahiya Emerick

A real textbook of Islamic Studies for use in grades 3-5. This textbook covers all the fundamentals of Islam and is arranged into clearly defined lessons and units. A stunningly beautiful book by the same author as the popular textbook for older children, "What Islam is All About." Illustrated, BW, 228 pages.